Golf Ball Chronicles

Another Vantage Press title by the author:

Body English

Golf Ball Chronicles

Fred Cisko

VANTAGE PRESS
New York

To all those women whose ambitions place them where few have been before, but where they, too, belong.

Author's Note

The author is not a writer. He is, however, a storyteller. Once again he brings you the story, you bring the imagination.

Golf Ball Chronicles

Chronicle One

Life is good. Although I do not participate much in the game of golf anymore, I watch every tournament my Master plays from my lofty position in his hatband. A few days later the whole family evaluates his performance via the video on the television screen in his trophy room. He earns big purses at every outing and has progressed to being one of the greatest golfers of all time. He needs me no more, his hole-in-one ace. Now I am his lucky charm. My body English has been more or less put out to pasture.

I have not been forgotten, however. My Master has published the story about my full-circle experiences through war and peace. It may someday prove to be a best seller. I go everywhere with him. We have attended countless banquets, testimonials and speaking engagements where he has held me high in the air amid much applause.

On one most memorable occasion we attended a prestigious golfing banquet which honored him. Luminaries from the sports and entertainment world were there as well as politicians from everywhere. The host was our good friend The Comedian, coming directly from Hollywood. He introduced my Master who then went on to speak about his last stroke ace-in-the-hole walk-off tournament win and my full-circle travels through the war and back to him. The audience was spellbound. Then the lights dimmed.

A mystery guest brought there by The Comedian walked in under spotlights. I started to shake. It was Mike, my Marine. When the lights went to full bright there was a hush in the audience, followed by a thundering applause and standing ovation.

If I knew how to faint, I would have. He was here, he was safe. In his full dress uniform he looked very impressive. Lieutenants bars were now on his shoulders and he was wearing a chest full of medals. He had been a hero several times over and won a battlefield commission. That may be a story for another day.

After being presented to the audience Mike filled in his part of my life in the war. He went on to say how I was grazed by a bullet and he took two rounds in his body armor from the same volley. Those in the banquet room were in awe. My Master seemed to be in total shock. I have never seen The Comedian so serious.

After Mike's speech he presented my Master and The Comedian each with one of the two bullets extracted from his armor on that frightful day. One could hear a pin drop in the banquet hall. After a few seconds of silence everyone rose and applauded respectfully.

When the speeches ended The Comedian and my Marine were invited to our home where Mike met the whole family. He made quite a hit especially with the children, Nancy and Gary. Mike also scored big time with Albatross. It was enlightening to see this big battle-hardened Marine making mushy mushy with a Beagle. No doubt he has a compassionate heart under his chest full of medals.

When he left that evening an emptiness enveloped me. Again I wondered if this would be the last time I would see him. Most certainly he would be back in the fight somewhere in the world. I pray our Creator watch over this good man and keep him safe.

My gift of motion and ever developing intellect have taken me on travels one could only imagine. I am continually learning about life and humans. Early on, just as I learned the game of golf by watching my Master's videos, I now watch current news events with all of the family.

During the nighttime sleeping hours I rest on my gold inscribed pedestal in the trophy room. The daytime hours find me with my Master wherever he goes. When the family relaxes during the evening I rest on the rug next to my Master's recliner. The only one who seems to know me for who I am is Albatross. He lies next to me, his nose inches away. At times his beady stare is telling me "I know all about you, but your secret is safe with me."

The family is very concerned over our country's involvement in the war in the Middle East. My early adventures and firsthand war experiences with my Marine leave me perplexed as to why this war thing has to happen at all. It seems to me with all of the knowledge mankind possesses throughout the world, if nations could just put their brightest people together every strife known to man could be eliminated and the world could live in peace, but what do I know? I'm just a golf ball. My ever-developing mind has not been programmed enough to evaluate the reasons for all this violence and hatred. Why is there not just one human family worldwide?

Kathy, my Master's wife, is especially upset. Before she and my Master married, she was an educator, a professor teaching government in a prestigious university. Her diplomas and documents of accomplishment adorn the walls of her office at home. She remains active and has become well known in humanitarian circles. She and my Master have traveled the world extensively, seeing the best and worst of it. Her great desire is to somehow, someday help those in the worst of it.

One evening Kathy and my Master attended a very nice dinner theater. Of course I went along. They enjoyed the meal and were pleased with the show. It was something about humans dressed like cats. Albatross would have been chasing them all over the stage.

As always, there were handshakes, "hello," and "nice to see you again" greetings from fans and well-wishers. Apparently it is well known that my Master takes me with him wherever he goes. There is always someone who wants to see "the ball" and my wound. He courteously shows me but he alone handles me. After my early traumatic experiences away from him I now feel totally safe.

After the show two professors who Kathy has known since her teaching days at the university stopped by our table. After pleasantries, they asked Kathy if she could attend a gathering of people in a few days. They jokingly said that if she wished she could leave her husband at home. Everybody laughed except me. Imagine, the king of golf and his ace were not invited.

After a few days passed, Kathy attended this gathering without us. Upon her return home she seemed overwhelmed. She went on to say that she was the main focus of the meeting which was actually a political gathering.

She related that after a period of discussion she was asked to be the party's candidate for a soon to be vacated seat in the U.S. Senate. It was obvious that her head was spinning. She did not give them an answer, wanting to talk it over with the family. She was pressed to come back with a decision within a few days.

Numerous family discussions took place. Both of the children were for it, but my Master was not so sure. Because of his golf prowess his family has always been in the spotlight—the positive spotlight. Politics can easily put one in a negative spotlight. My Master knows that Kathy

4

can handle anything that comes her way; his concern is for the children and their exposure to it all. Within himself he knows that she really wants this. He struggled with what was best for her and the family.

On the third day of decision the family went to dinner at our favorite restaurant. After a quiet meal my Master asked Kathy if she had made a decision. Her answer was "No." After a pause, he raised his wine glass to her and said, "Go for it." There was total silence then all of the family had tears of joy in their eyes—including me.

In two seconds I am firmly in my Master's hand; he gives me a loving, thankful look, a kiss, and passes me over to Kathy. He tells her that I will bring as much luck as I have brought him and to keep me close. I know that my life with my family is about to change once again.

Keeping me close became a logistical problem for a time. The realization is that most clothing made for women is not adaptable to carrying a golf ball. A necklace I cannot be, nor a bracelet, nor a ring or a set of earrings, nor a pair of high heels.

My Master decided to take me back to our family jeweler from where I was stolen during a burglary in the early morning hours. From there I found myself on an incredible journey in what now seems to be another lifetime. His thought is that the jeweler may be able to devise a fitting of some kind. My thought is that I don't want to go. Bad memories of crime and thievery at this place haunt me. The possibility of losing my family again is upsetting.

Fortunately Kathy and my Master took me to our jeweler and watched as I was fitted with a removable harness made out of plastic as a pattern. The final version would be of light stainless steel with a sturdy clip which would secure me to Kathy's clothing or handbag. I did not have to stay overnight which made me very happy. We returned a few days later for the final fitting. Now I am good to go.

Chronicle Two

My Master is on his own now, playing tournaments without his ace along for luck. Kathy, on the political trail, is making her mark.

The party that declared her their candidate became a little upset with her. She declared her run for the Senate seat in a way no one has ever done before for any office. She hates the financial part of the campaign and the millions of dollars in donations it takes to run one. She feels that this money can be better utilized on meaningful programs that benefit the poor and homeless. Veterans benefits could also be enhanced with the donations collected, especially disabled combat veterans.

She declared to her party that she would announce a platform which asked for the vote in her party's primary of everyone who feels as she does. She planned to hold all donations in an account to be later shared by all of the needy whether or not she wins the nomination. She is fervent in her belief that all those millions of dollars in contributions could benefit real people in unlimited ways. Her party's image in the eyes of the country could be greatly enhanced as well, but to her that was secondary.

When the party fathers explored this unique approach they were divided. Did they choose the right person to represent them? After argument, discussion and some reservations they envisioned that this could be a good political tactic after all.

When it was announced to the media it proved to be a blockbuster. It was the talk of the country. Kathy's efforts received media coverage that money could not buy. Donations came in from everywhere. Small amounts of one dollar from interested school children to thousands of dollars from a multitude of sources poured in. Letters accompanied many donations. People were thrilled with the idea that their money would help others directly. The party's membership rose dramatically with new voters registering by the hundreds. The party fathers were ecstatic.

The following months were grueling. We did not see the family as much as we would have liked. All of the family at one time or another participated in public campaign appearances including my Master. It was nice to see that he did not try to overshadow Kathy, not that he could have at this point. She was on a roll and was the darling of the political world. Her position on issues made sense. Her views were reasonable. Most of all, she exuded honesty.

She won the challenges of her party's primary and went on to win the Senate seat by a landslide. She is now Senator-Elect and I was part of it—a golf ball with body English held in reserve.

Swearing in ceremonies are on the horizon and we are off to Washington, the seat of our government. On the flight my thoughts drift back to the new sporting goods store, where I was given to my Master, and then my first airplane ride. It seems so long ago.

The whole family is together now, even Albatross. He has traveled by air many times and is on the floor under the seat in his zipped-up carrier.

The following day Kathy took her oath of office. The President and Vice-President of the United States were there as well as every Senator and Congressperson. All of the Supreme Court Justices were present, some of whom were participating in the swearing in of the newly elected officials.

When Kathy raised her right hand I was clasped to the shoulder strap of her handbag. I was closer to the ceremony than the rest of the family. In fact, I made national television when the camera at one point zeroed in on ME.

Kathy looked beautiful. Her suit was neat, plain and business-like. She was radiant and glowed as bright as a new penny. Afterward there was a reception, the likes of which I have never seen.

At the end of the evening we returned to the hotel exhausted. My furry friend was full of life having spent the evening in our room sleeping. His only interruption was a young lady who the hotel provided to walk him during our absence. His exuberance upon our return calmed down when everyone went to bed.

The next day Kathy was shown her office. It was the same one her predecessor had occupied. When newly elected officials take over they are given the option of keeping their offices as they are or completely redecorating and refurbishing them. Kathy opted to leave them as they are—good for her. She couldn't see changing perfectly good furnishings and décor because it didn't suit her taste, government waste and all. There will be no pork barrel projects connected to her.

Kathy and I have very nice living quarters in a brownstone near the Capitol. It is a short commute daily to her office. Once again life is good. I am learning much about the inner workings of government.

I feel a little out of my element. I miss my Master and the game of golf. Through our early playing days we really bonded. Those days I long for—his association with the players and the fans, especially the fans. They love him, and me of course.

Kathy was invited to sit on the prestigious and powerful Senate Foreign Relations Committee, taking the seat of her predecessor. After several weeks passed, she had many unanswered questions about the conflict in the Middle East.

As part of her duties on this committee her feeling is that she should go to the war zone and evaluate our country's involvement for herself.

Uneasiness grips me now just as it must for all those servicemen and women, many with children who are being deployed there. I can only imagine the vacuum left in the hearts of all when a loved one goes off to war. I clearly remember Mike's family coming apart on the day my Marine was recalled for deployment while on his thirty-day leave. That was a heartwrenching time for everyone. In the morning we were playing golf. In the afternoon we were off to war. That was then, this is now, but the fear and worrying never subsides. It is always there.

On the day Kathy and I were leaving for the war zone our whole family arrived to see us off. It was good to see my Master. There were a few tears. My Master told Kathy to keep me close for luck. One other new senator and three new members of the House of Representatives were also going.

I was the only one who had been there before and I must say if I had knees I would be weak-kneed. The only one of the group who had experienced war was Kathy's fellow senator. He is a graduate of the United States Naval Academy at Annapolis and was one of the first black midshipmen to rise to the top of his graduating class. He served as a naval fighter pilot during a previous conflict and after many combat missions he had an engine failure over enemy territory and had to bail out. He was captured and suffered the indignities of being beaten and starved. He was held prisoner until the end of the conflict and returned as a shadow of the man who left. During his rehabilitation he was determined to bring himself back to where he was mentally and physically and he did. Like Kathy, he wanted to see this war for himself and get some direct answers.

Our flight to the Middle East was uneventful. Approaching Europe we picked up a fighter escort which accompanied us to Germany. Once there our airplane was refueled while everyone stretched. Body English works well after a long flight. We were given a military meal among many servicemen and women. As always there were questions about me, the famous golf ball. Kathy had me securely clamped to her handbag and she never fails to mention that I am her lucky charm. I feel good about that.

Before leaving Germany everyone was fitted with customized military clothing and protective gear. Kathy's handbag was retired temporarily. I was now clamped to her helmet goggle strap. On my first tour of duty I had been in that position with my Marine so this perch is nothing new for me.

From Germany another fighter escort accompanied us to the Middle East where we landed in the so-called "safe zone" of the conflict. During the next two days we attended a series of meetings with military personnel from generals to foot soldiers. I am amazed at the dedication and determination of these men and women.

After careful thought and evaluation, our Congress people requested to go out on a real patrol. There was a flurry of communication between the military people and

Washington. Ultimately the request was granted. We were to be embedded within a mission.

The military needed one day to gear up. This required our attending an orientation session to familiarize us with what we may encounter out on patrol. This orientation was conducted by a colonel. When it was over he brought in the battle group that was going to run the patrol and protect us.

The first one introduced was the lieutenant in command. I couldn't believe it. It was Mike, my Marine. He looked directly at Kathy, putting military protocol aside, and winked. I winked back but I don't think he caught it. There must have been quite a bit of string pulling between the military and Washington to have Mike and his men assigned to us. Nobody asked—nobody said. He introduced all of his marines and where they were from.

After the introductions Mike came over and Kathy threw her arms around him with a big hug. His face blushed red. The other marines looked puzzled but then realized that they knew each other. Kathy pointed to me and her explanation of my presence brought everything in line. Mike gave me a loving squeeze with his big fist. I was back in the Marine Corps.

The next two days were scheduled as our patrol days. One patrol lasting about four hours was set for each day. We would be looking for insurgent activity or any indication of it. Orders were not to engage the enemy unless circumstances required defending ourselves. The mission was to observe and report back.

Our route was carefully laid out. It would be closely monitored from above by pilotless drone aircraft. The patrol consisted of six humvees. Three marines and one official were in each vehicle. Mike assigned Kathy to his vehicle. The lead vehicle contained only marines. Kathy's fellow senator was in the second vehicle and we were the third in line. The others followed. Everyone was heavily armed except the officials.

Once out of the "safe zone" compound we were enveloped into another world. There were bombed-out homes, blown-up and burned-out vehicles, and people wandering about aimlessly.

We passed many who held up jugs and pots for water. We could not stop. Many wore outer garments which covered them from neck to ankle. Underneath that garment could be an automatic weapon or an explosive vest. It is hard to tell an enemy from a friendly. Kathy was very quiet. Mike sat close to her on one side and his radio man was on the other. I felt like I was part of a marine sandwich.

Some of those we passed waved, some stared defiantly and others just looked away. The devastation this war has caused is overwhelming. The civilian loss of life has to be staggering. If I had a heart it would be bleeding for all those innocent people killed, maimed and crippled by this conflict—especially the children.

Several times our humvees were hit by stones, the thrower of which was never seen.

The first day's patrol was quiet. We returned well before dusk. The marines went for a briefing and the officials went for a military meal with the troops. Of course, I went along.

Kathy retired early but spent a restless night. I can only imagine what went through her mind. My thoughts drift back to my Master and our family. What must they be thinking and how much must they be worrying?

The next morning we went for breakfast with Mike and his marines. They ate heartily as most combat soldiers do, not knowing when or where their next meal would be or if they would be alive to have one.

After we saddled up in the humvees we were on our way. Today a different route was planned, the landscape being more barren. About two hours out radio communications notified us that there could be hostility along our way. About three hours into the patrol Mike was notified of an immediate threat up ahead. He increased the speed of the convoy.

Off to our right was a low rocky ridge line. Behind this ridge was a gathering of possible insurgents. Our drone aircraft picked them up on its video scanner. Within a minute or so we came under intense small arms fire. Then the worst happened. A rocket propelled grenade exploded in front of the #2 vehicle which contained Kathy's senator colleague. The humvee was disabled and the driver was seriously wounded. The convoy was forced to stop.

Mike immediately had his radio man call for an air strike on the ridge and inform the base of our situation. Within seconds our humvee was hit and disabled by another explosive device. Everyone had to get out.

Kathy was as cool as could be. She knew enough to stick with Mike. Small arms fire peppered the ground around us but Mike managed to herd all of us behind the humvee for cover.

Within a minute or two Kathy's senator colleague came running toward us carrying the unconscious driver of his vehicle. He was also shouldering the wounded marine's automatic rifle. The rest of the marines and the marines in the lead vehicle were dug in and returning fire.

He put the wounded marine, who was bleeding from a chest wound, on the ground next to Kathy. Mike shielded both of them with his body as best he could while returning fire. Kathy immediately tended to the wounded marine. She was successful in stopping the flow of blood by applying heavy pressure to the wound even as she exposed herself to enemy fire. Mike asked the senator if he was familiar with the use of the weapon he was holding. His reply was "Absolutely." Mike said, "Good—pick a target." Without any hesitation he did and helped defend us.

Shortly after hundreds of rounds of ammunition were expended by both sides three helicopters arrived and the fight was over. Two of them were gunships and they annihilated the ridge, insurgents and all.

Our people piled into the four remaining humvees. Mike ordered the third chopper, an ambulance type, to land on the road to pick up their wounded comrade. Kathy held pressure on the marine's chest until he was loaded into the chopper and medical personnel took over. She refused the pilot's offer to fly back with them. The chopper then headed to the base at full speed.

The two other choppers flew cover for us but one delayed long enough to destroy the disabled humvees preventing further use of any kind by the enemy. During the run back Mike noticed that there was a considerable amount of blood over Kathy's face and neck. The blood was not from the marine she tended to, it was hers. She caught a small piece of shrapnel in her left cheek just ahead of her left earlobe. She told Mike that she didn't feel it at all. This must be where the adrenaline kicks in. Mike dressed the wound from the vehicle's medical kit and radioed ahead for medical assistance upon arrival. He knew the shrapnel would have to be probed for and removed surgically. The wound had closed.

Upon returning to the "safe zone" medics met us and we were off to the hospital. Mike, his men and Kathy's senator colleague were off to a briefing.

Chronicle Three

In the hospital, if you can call it that, there was a flurry of activity. Doctors and military brass were all over us. The media had gotten word of the firefight and were straining for information.

Also, word of the situation had somehow reached my Master. He was on a quickly rigged portable military telephone hookup at Kathy's bedside within minutes. She convinced him that she was in no pain and that his ace—that's me—brought her the luck that he said I would. The shrapnel could have easily lodged in her eye or her neck and throat, but it didn't.

After a few minutes military doctors declared that the operating section was ready. She hung up with an "I love you." Kathy's only request was that I accompany her during the operation. Military doctors are accustomed to wounded personnel being attached to a good luck charm and wanting to have it with them. Her request was quickly granted and I was clamped to the front of her bra strap—of all places.

During the operation she was put under with anesthesia, but I watched everything. These doctors are excellent. My learning curve is increasing rapidly. The piece of shrapnel they removed was about the size of an elongated nickel and as thick. It is hard to believe that she never felt it.

When we returned to the ward where her hospital

bed was located Mike and Kathy's senator colleague were there as well as all the other Congressional representatives who were in the battle. Everyone applauded. Word traveled fast to the other wounded service people in the ward. Her efforts in saving the life of a wounded marine while being exposed to enemy fire and being wounded herself spread quickly. The left side of her face sported a good-sized bandage and was quite swollen.

The doctors came in shortly thereafter and presented her with the piece of shrapnel they removed. She considered it her new lucky charm. My Master was back on the military phone hookup and was a bit unnerved to say the least. Between Kathy and her doctors he was assured that the operation went well and she would be fine. A little plastic surgery was in her future.

Kathy and I now have something in common—a battle scar. Mine is from my first tour of duty. I must say the circumstances surrounding both wounds were very scary.

The news media saturated this makeshift hospital but Kathy would give no interviews. The military people were very good at keeping them at a distance. Before Kathy left the hospital she visited other wounded personnel and thanked them for their sacrifice and devotion to duty. The first one she visited was the wounded marine whose life she saved. He was conscious and well aware of what she had done. They had a pleasant conversation and he thanked her over and over. She leaned down and kissed him on the cheek. I had tears in my eyes, wherever they are. His doctor told her that because of her quick action in stopping the flow of blood this marine would recover nicely, otherwise he would have been gone.

Kathy was released the next day joining all of her colleagues for meetings with the newly elected officials of this war-torn country's government. They were hoping to gain a perspective on the war and our country's involvement in it. They came away informed but not satisfied.

After the day-long meetings everyone was looking forward to reflection and relaxation. That period did not last long. During the evening meal we were notified that our contingent would be leaving at midnight.

Departures are scheduled during all hours of the day and night. The military people decided that leaving under the cover of darkness would present less of a target for shoulder-fired missiles and such. Several large transport jets would take off at the same time making it confusing for the enemy to target a single one. Because of the media coverage our presence was known worldwide.

Mike and his men met us at the boarding ramp. He gave Kathy a bear hug and me a squeeze with that big fist. I thought I heard him say, "You're discharged." If he didn't say it, I felt it.

I wondered when I would see him again. Our Creator has kept him safe. Please let his safety continue. Let all of these servicemen and women who are serving their country so unselfishly come home safely and soon to their families.

At exactly midnight we were airborne along with two other military cargo jets. Once in the air four fighters moved into position to escort us to Germany. After landing our group changed to civilian clothes and we had our last meal with the troops. Kathy created quite a stir. The left side of her face was bandaged and still swollen. I really didn't know how she felt, but I felt proud of her. Here is a woman, not in the military, requesting to be put in harm's way and measuring up big time when harm came.

The media somehow from a distance, snapped several photos of her and her bandaged face. These pictures were on the front page of newspapers worldwide even before we arrived home. The story of her saving the life of a wounded marine and her senator colleague not hesitating to join in the fight with the wounded marine's weapon made for compelling reading. Both are truly heroes.

The flight from Germany to the United States was relaxing. About five hundred miles out our pilot came over the intercom telling us that we were in for a special treat. We were going to be welcomed home by the Blue Angels, the navy's fighter jet precision acrobatic team. We were not aware of it at the time, but Kathy's senator colleague was part of that group early in his naval career. Apparently after media word of his recent exploits, the team wanted to welcome home one of their own.

Our pilot told us that their commander requested he hold our big jet straight and level. He expected an up in your face greeting telling us not to be alarmed if they came in close.

First they passed quite slowly and close enough for us to clearly see them smile and wave. During the next pass they were inverted and a little above us each holding a sign in the cockpit which was right side up which read "Welcome Home." During the third pass they came by slowly just waving with a thumbs up salute, except for the last one. He came by with a big bandage stuck on his cheek for Kathy and was throwing kisses with both hands. I wondered who was flying the airplane. Our group laughed and waved back.

After that they pulled their noses up, cranked in the afterburners and seemed to be orbit bound. Kathy's senator colleague was choked up with emotion. It was then that he told us that he was once part of that group. There could not have been a more fitting or wonderful greeting.

When we landed the families of the legislators were waiting at the ramp. So were the six pilots of the Blue Angels. They stood near the bottom of the ramp at attention in a hand salute. With their other hand they held the "Welcome Home" sign they displayed in the cockpit during the flight. Of course with their awesome speed they beat us in. Their jets were parked side by side in a line facing us as we came down the ramp. All of the Blue Angels support team were standing at attention lined up in front of their airplanes. I was truly impressed.

After handshakes and hugs with the other Congressmen Kathy hugged her senator colleague. She said to him, "It is gratifying to know our country has warriors like you." He graciously nodded and said, "Thanks, I'll see you at the podium."

Our family left the base by limousine going directly to Reagan National Airport where we boarded a commercial flight home, garnering much attention. My Master would not let go of Kathy's hand. He had many questions, but put them off for another day. She was very quiet. At times there was a sadness in her eyes. No doubt she was reflecting on her past ten days.

When we arrived at our door the whole family was in a more or less somber mood. We came out of it when Albatross was released from his carrier. He tore through the house with Blue Angels speed checking out every room. He was happy to be home and was doing his best to make a nuisance of himself.

There was time now for family togetherness. My Master was between tours, the children were out of school and Congress was in summer session. The wheels of government turn slowly in the summertime.

On my Master's birthday the family went to dinner at our favorite restaurant. Just before dessert the servers gathered at our table and sang the birthday song. They presented him with a large strawberry cake covered with mounds of whipped cream. Kathy handed him a small neatly wrapped and ribboned box. I was inside. As he jiggled the box while opening it he perpetuated my motion. When the top came off I gathered all the body English I could muster and jumped out, landing in the middle of the whipped cream. Everyone laughed hysterically. Kathy told him the luck I brought her was being returned. My Master wiped me off, gave me a kiss and said, "Thanks."

Kathy then showed the family her new lucky charm. She had the piece of shrapnel which was lodged in her cheek gold plated and inscribed with the date, time and location of the battle. It was now a part of a necklace hanging from a gold chain. It was fashioned by our family jeweler who as you know has a long history with us. Kathy put it on and said that she would wear it always, even when wearing other necklaces.

Chronicle Four

Life is even better now. I am back with my family and on tour with my Master and the game of golf.

Kathy went back to her senatorial duties. It seemed to her that in a very short time honesty and truthfulness have left the arena in Washington. Arrogance and indifference have remained. She was going to do her best to change that. The age-old view that my party is always right even when it is wrong was going to be attacked. She felt that sincere bipartisanship could realize true purpose and direction if legislators could be honest with themselves.

She immediately set out to persuade legislators to do what is right for the American people regardless of the political party they represent. If it meant that they should disagree with the party hardliners over an obvious wrong, do so, and don't try to sugarcoat it. Also, politicians being in denial of a situation did not set well with her.

The first one to openly agree with her was her wartime senator colleague and friend. He represented the opposition party but like Kathy was convinced that party allegiance was secondary to the good of the people. Both are steadfast in their belief that in a democracy the voice of the people was meant to count.

As time progressed there was truly more bipartisanship. The halls of Congress were starting to reflect the real voice of the people. Lobbyists were having a fit. Big money coupled with political influence was slowly fading away.

Party spokespeople were no longer spinning a cloak of deception to mask mistakes and ineptness. Legislators were recognizing the value of Kathy's thinking. The so-called "middle class" was back with a voice.

These new political views were filtering into state and local politics. Kathy was changing the political landscape of the country. Her sincerity and honesty have risen well above political subterfuge.

While my Master and I are back on tour, Kathy's mother, now living with us, is in charge of the day to day activities of the household. The children are back in school and their grandmother has become Kathy's watchful eye. Kathy's schedule allows her to fly home most weekends.

Albatross is the only one who was a little upset with this arrangement. I guess he felt that if there were going to be a new boss in the house it should be him. He sulked around for a day or so but grandmother being an excellent cook easily won him over. Beagles will do anything for food—-even stop sulking and behave.

As time went on my Master and I played golf and Kathy legislated. Her attendance record is better than anyone. She never misses a meeting, a session or a vote. She speaks her mind and no political rhetoric. Her integrity is like a breath of fresh air in Washington.

A new summer season is nearing and my Master has agreed to play in the British Open in England. He has played this before but has never won. Fortunately Kathy would be on summer vacation and decided to go along. Grandmother will keep an eye on the children and Albatross will be on household guard duty and oversee everything, or so he thinks.

Kathy requested through official government channels a meeting with the British Prime Minister. His views on the war and a one on one discussion would mean much to her. He accepted her request. The media was quick to cover our departure. Kathy's meeting with the Prime Minister and my Master's attempt to win the British Open made for worthwhile coverage.

On our flight over, attendants, flight personnel and travelers could not have been more pleasant. The King of Golf, a wounded U.S. senator and a lucky charm golf ball are quite a curiosity.

After the plastic surgery on Kathy's war wound there is a small scar on her left cheek. In time, according to the doctors, the scar will fade. People are kind enough not to stare and Kathy is not self-conscious about it at all.

My Master is pleased that she is along. At least now, with each always having busy schedules, they can be together on somewhat of a vacation even though it is work for both of them. I am happy to be a part of it.

Going through customs is something new for me. Upon entering another country I am used to blasting in on a military jet and out the same way. Being scrutinized from every angle and passing through electronic and x-ray screening seems somewhat intense. I'll bet they can see my little rubber heart.

My Master and Kathy had to answer numerous questions from the customs people. Their status meant nothing to the agents. I wonder how many people, if any, walk into England without being checked. That may be another story for another day.

Kathy was not scheduled to meet with the Prime Minister for two days, therefore she could attend the opening of the classic. She would spend the third day with the Prime Minister and then together they would attend the final day of the tournament. I'll bet they get good seats.

The evening before the match we went to a very nice welcoming party for all the players. Dignitaries as well as players were anxious to meet Kathy. My Master mused at the fact that he is now overshadowed by his famous wife. If people knew of my body English story I would over-shadow both of them. My secret is still safe with Alba-tross. Until some genius converts his woofing into the English language, I am probably okay.

The day the tournament started, notables from all walks of life and fans from all over the world attended. There were thousands in the gallery. Most were well dressed as if they were going to a wedding. This is England.

I feel secure on my perch in my Master's hatband. As you know he is famous for his wide-brimmed golfing hat and his lucky charm—me—in his hatband.

My Master started off with powerful and accurate drives. His irons were also accurate and I must say crafty. He knows exactly which iron to use for the stroke at hand. His putts were deadly. We finished well ahead on the first day.

That evening we had a quiet dinner where Kathy re-lated that she was a little nervous about her upcoming meeting with the Prime Minister. My Master assured her that after all she had accomplished as a U.S. senator in changing the political thinking in our country she could handle anything that crossed her path with the Prime Minister.

The second day of golf was much like the first. My Master had a good day. We ended the day well in the lead.

He was rock solid having confidence and resolve. I saw no hesitation or uncertainty in his focus. It seemed to me that he had come to win.

I will never forget our one stroke ace win and my diving wingover into the cup capping a tournament that had always eluded him on the last hole. He had hit me too hard, too low and too fast from the tee, but providence provided us with a walk off ace and we won it. That was then, this is now. Things could change drastically in the game of golf, but if I knew how to bet, I would bet the farm on him.

The third day Kathy went to see the Prime Minister. She said that he was cordial and explained Great Britain's role in the conflict. He also explained the reasons for his country's planned withdrawal. The general public in England wants its participation to end. The House of Commons does as well. If that happens our country will be in the fight virtually alone. Our armed forces will be stretched beyond what is reasonable. Kathy was not happy with that projection. She fully recognizes that there are overall benchmark failures on our part in this war that are irrevocable. For her this is disheartening.

After her visit she was escorted to a session of the House of Commons and another in the House of Lords.

Kathy was amused at the intense level of open and brash discord connected with delegates in both houses. Perhaps their legislators have something to learn about decorum from us "colonials" after all.

On the third day when Kathy was with the Prime Minister we played well. My Master hit a few balls which were off his mark but he recovered nicely without getting flustered.

So many golfers will go into a slump and take weeks to come out of it. I think that most of the time their problem is more mental than physical, much like a batting slump in that wild game of baseball. I know, I am prejudiced toward my game of golf. One must agree, though, that it is a respectful game, where fans do not scream or curse at the players, or taunt them with obscene gestures.

One thing I observed in all games that use a ball is that the poor ball is clubbed, batted, thrown, kicked, paddled, swatted or pounded on the floor. We get no credit or praise for this—but here I am humanizing us. My vivid imagination tells me that maybe we should form a union of some kind. What a shocker that would be.

On this third day we were on the 10th green. I saw a strange move made by a ball rolling in a long putt by a British golfer. The ball was well off the cup but made a sharp almost right angle turn and went in. To the gallery, it looked as if it may have hit a pebble or something to deflect it and make it change direction. There was no pebble or obvious obstruction. The gallery gasped at the sight. Could there be another ball in existence with body English like mine? If so, could we possibly communicate? There goes my crazy imagination again, but in the future I will watch closely.

The evening before the last day of play we went to dinner early. My Master wanted to retire early and get a good night's sleep. Kathy tried not to let her more or less stressful day affect him. She told him only that her day went well with the Prime Minister. Even though my Master was well ahead she wanted all his concentration to be on his game and not on her, politics, the war or anything else.

In the morning the Prime Minister arrived in a limousine to escort Kathy to the game. My Master walked her to the car and met the Prime Minister whom he liked instantly. I liked him too. He had a quick sense of humor.

Through a three or four minute conversation he had us all laughing—even me. He even laughed at himself. There is something genuine about a person who can laugh at himself. Kathy left my Master with a kiss for good luck, telling him that she would see him on the green at the last hole.

Kathy related to us later what happened next. Upon arrival in the area of the last green she and the Prime Minister were quickly escorted from his vehicle to front row seats beyond the outer perimeter of the green. Security was everywhere. There was a quiet party-like atmosphere among all of the spectators.

The golfers were playing a few holes back. Their progress was being monitored on several television screens around the green which would be removed before play on the final hole began. There was assigned seating and Kathy wondered why there was an empty seat in the front row between her and the Prime Minister, but didn't give it much thought. Everyone was pleasant and aware of Kathy's presence.

After a few minutes, there was a flurry of activity a short distance away and a hush came over the gallery. Everyone rose as the Queen of England appeared. She motioned everyone to be seated and then took her seat between the Prime Minister and Kathy. A respectful applause arose from the gallery. Kathy was fascinated. Sitting next to The Queen was breathtaking for her. She found The Queen to be very down to earth. The Queen was also interested in Kathy's war experience and wanted to see the piece of shrapnel Kathy had made into a necklace. She never asked to see her wound but Kathy pointed to it when relating her experiences. The Queen was moved and commended Kathy for her bravery.

My Master and I knew nothing of this as we approached the last and final hole. He was well in the lead and needed only four strokes for par. We did it in three and it was over. Upon approaching the green my Master never looked for Kathy. He knew she was there but was concentrating on his game. He wanted to finish it as solidly as he started and played it.

Now that it was over his eyes found her in the front row of the gallery sitting with The Queen of England and her Prime Minister. They were applauding vigorously. He was flabbergasted at the sight.

After the din of applause died down, the three walked over to my Master and The Queen presented him with a large gold cup inscribed with the win. My Master was overwhelmed with emotion. He really didn't know what to do with his hands or feet feeling very self-conscious in the presence of The Queen. Clumsily, he took a sort of half step backward and tripped over his putter. There was a muffled giggle from the gallery. When my Master righted himself and not knowing what else to do or say he handed his putter to The Queen and said, "It's yours, your Highness." She said, "Thank you, I will put it to good use."

The Queen then invited us to Buckingham Palace the next day for tea and a private tour. The Prime Minister and his wife were also invited. It is hard for me to believe that I am here witnessing all this pomp and royalty.

The next day a limousine appeared and we were off to see The Queen. The Prime Minister and his wife met us in the courtyard and The Queen's Guard escorted us in. Tea turned out to be a small banquet.

The Queen was quite cordial. Her manner and bearing was certainly that of royalty, but she was not stuffy or aloof. The highlight for me was when she told my Master that she had read the book he had published about me and my early experiences. She is really current on things.

My Master promptly produced me. He showed her where I was grazed by a bullet in the war and the identifying marks he placed on me after our hole-in-one tournament win. She was amazed to learn that none of my experiences were fiction. My ending up back with my Master after all of my travels was mind-boggling to her. It still is to me, too.

The Queen is the only one except our family that my Master has let hold me. I felt as if I were knighted. I stayed absolutely still while in her hand hoping that in my excitement my body English would not overcome me and produce a wiggle or a squirm in her hand. She would have had the fright of her life.

During our visit The Queen told Kathy that she admired her determination and resolve at putting new life into the political system in our country. She also said that she can foresee monumental things happening for Kathy. That is quite an acknowledgment coming from The Queen of England.

The Queen has a sense of humor as well, asking my Master if he has tripped over any golf clubs since yesterday. Everyone broke up laughing.

Somehow overnight, she had my Master's putter gold plated and inscribed. She told him to get it into his trophy room before he hurt himself with it. Imagine that, The Queen being a jokestress. She's my kind of lady and I say that most respectfully.

The next day we toured Windsor Castle. To say that it is an impressive and formidable structure is a mild description. It is a massive fortification and probably the premier fortification of its time. Within the castle, the walls of its corridors, rooms and halls display thousands of swords, bows, arrows, lances, shields, body armor and every battle implement used to wage war in hand to hand combat in the days of the Crusades and the Knights of the Round Table. The rooms are furnished with treasures from the Royal Collection, including paintings by famous artists, tapestries and sculptures. Anyone who has never visited England should plan to do so. To see this structure and what it holds for visitors is awesome.

When we left the Queen asked us to visit her again the next time we are in England. I hope we do. Our visit with her was most pleasurable. She was absolutely de-lightful.

Chronicle Five

Our flight back to the United States was more or less uneventful. We have truly become celebrities. My Master is
used to it but Kathy is not. The news media can be quite
overbearing. She doesn't appreciate a camera or a micro-
phone being pushed in her face unexpectedly. That was
the case at the airport, but she handled it well.

We should have Mike, my Marine, as our bodyguard.
His size and seemingly mild manner would make any media person back off and think twice about what might
trigger this fighting machine into action. There I go
again, thinking about him. I hope he is well and Providence is good to him wherever he is.

On our flight several well-wishers and golf fans con-
gratulated my Master with his win. They acknowledged
Kathy and were very respectful of her. They kept their
distance.

Upon landing and clearing customs the media was
waiting like foxes at the henhouse door. Pre-arranged security whisked us away to board another flight home. Everyone slept most of the way. When we arrived home
Kathy's mom, the children and Albatross met us at the
airport. That goofy dog was so glad to see us I thought he
was going to crawl inside my Master's shirt. He was even
glad to see me. He pushed his wet nose into my Master's
hatband as a greeting but I put my body English into motion and squirmed away before he decided to get his fangs

on me. Nobody noticed except Albatross. I outsmarted him again.

Shortly after we returned home a letter arrived from Mike. It was addressed to my Master. My recent thoughts of him must have sent him a mental message. He apologized for not writing sooner and wanted to relate how brave Kathy was during their firefight. He went on to say that she represented her country well and was adored by the troops. The opinion is his small part of the military is that she should make a run for the Presidency. They feel that she would make a fine Commander-in-Chief. He jokingly went on to write that if my Master ever wanted to give her up, he would marry her in a heartbeat. Kathy and my Master had fun with that. It was good to see that he was well and in good humor.

My Master wrote back and mailed off a dozen of his published books about my life and travels. Wow! My notoriety is really getting around. No doubt my story will be read by many of our troops and I feel honored by that.

A month or so later my Master and I went to Washington for the weekend to visit Kathy and take in the sights. She wanted to show us our country's Capitol on her two days off. Most of the legislators go home for the weekend so the halls of Congress are relatively empty.

Saturday was busy. We visited landmarks and monuments. We paid our respects at the Tomb of the Unknown Solider from World War One. We visited the graves where hundreds of the fallen in our wars are laid to rest. That was a very moving experience for all of us.

Sunday morning we went to Kathy's office in the Senate building. She wanted to pick up some material to study after we leave for home later in the day. Her upcoming week was scheduled to be a busy one. She wanted to be prepared and informed.

Shortly after we arrived in the building security alarms flashed and sounded. Everyone inside was required to leave immediately. Security procedures automatically fall into place in these situations. Capitol Police, Secret Service and FBI personnel appear out of nowhere and inform those leaving what to do next. The building is then cleared methodically.

Apparently there was a threat of some kind on Washington and the whole city was shut down. Kathy would let no one separate her from my Master. She told the law enforcement people to take her wherever they liked, but her husband goes too. No one wanted to challenge her so off we went—including me.

I will not divulge what followed or where we were taken because of national security. All of the legislators who were still in Washington were quickly accounted for and protected.

The numerous law enforcement agencies connected with this exercise are first class. They are dedicated people willing to put their life on the line to protect not only the legislators but the public at large.

Everything went smoothly. Every measure of safety and comfort under the circumstances was well thought out and implemented. My life experiences never cease to bewilder me. I have already been shot at and hit, but I certainly do not want to be blown up, as little as I am, if that is the threat. Even my body English wouldn't be able to save me.

The threat persisted throughout the day as well as the next. The news media was clamoring for information. If anyone had it, they were not forthcoming.

Fortunately, this being the weekend, a good number of legislators were at home. They were notified not to come back to Washington until cleared to do so but to stay available for procedural notifications. It was fortunate that they were not together in a centralized location which could, I suppose, present a desirable target. I am sure, however, that there are provisions in place for that eventuality as well.

The threat lasted two days. The whole country was put on alert. It turned out that satellite surveillance detected a massive cylindrical vehicle of some kind moving along the Atlantic Ocean floor about 1,000 miles east of Washington heading steadily and slowly toward our shores. It was tracked for several hours. Before our naval experts could get into position for an evaluation, it vanished. The Navy searched the area repeatedly but came up with nothing.

Underwater experts and scientists were hosted by the Navy to participate in the search. Underwater photographic and recovery vehicles of all types were sent down on the last known position of the object. Nothing was found except that the ocean floor had been greatly disturbed over a large area at that location. The puzzling part is that it was there, then it was gone, much like the so-called and elusive flying saucers observed worldwide for years which seem to come and go at will.

The news media was pressing for answers, but there were none. Moreover, the public was upset because they felt there was a government cover-up, reminiscent of the suspected cover-up of the alien flying-saucer incident at Roswell, New Mexico years ago. No one could accept the fact that this large object disappeared without a trace. The country was in a controlled panic mode. Eventually the furor died down and things returned to normal. People calmed down and everyday life came back on line.

Lingering, however, was the haunting question of what this thing could be. If at this point anyone knew, no one was saying. Samples were taken of the disturbed ocean floor. The results were inconclusive, according to government spokespeople. It looks as if the country has another Roswell on its hands.

Chronicle Six

Every year women's organizations worldwide come together in a seminar to rally support and direction for
women who strive for goals never dreamed of in earlier
decades.

Attending are women from all walks of life, the corpo-
rate world, education, politics, the military, law enforcement, the news media and the medical field to mention a
few. Women's place in the world, their accomplishments
and their acceptance have come to the forefront as never
before. This venue promotes and encourages all of them
to step up and make a difference. There is an untapped
reservoir of intelligence and foresight deep within all
women straining to be unleashed. Even from my limited
golf ball perspective I wonder if the world were controlled
by women, who give birth to children and are the main-
stays of their rearing, would they be so quick to send them
off to war to slaughter and be slaughtered? Perhaps rea-
soning and common sense would prevail and male muscle
flexing and posturing would be diminished somewhat. I
can easily make these judgments without prejudice in
that I am neither a male or a female—just a golf ball with
an ever increasing intellect and an overabundance of
common sense.

The gathering this year is being held in Las Vegas
where there is entertainment and relaxation for all during the off hours. Scores of workshops are provided for all

those who have special interests in specific fields. Every base is touched to make women feel more comfortable and confident within themselves as well as in the world around them.

Kathy was invited to be a speaker during the political segment of this conclave. Even with all her pressing senatorial commitments she felt compelled to accept.

She told us later that all went well with her presentation. Of course during her question and answer period her war experiences were addressed.

Kathy never gave any specific interviews to the media about her participation in the fight. Questions brought that out. The audience was spellbound. She left the podium with a standing ovation.

Overall she was pleased with the amount of women attending. Women from all over the world were there, many from so-called third world countries. It was enlightening for her to see the degree of interest in every presentation given by other dignitaries. She feels that she and other women are making a difference in the world but there is still much work to do.

While attending this seminar Kathy met a high ranking female Border Patrol agent who was attending the law segment of the seminar. The agent invited Kathy to visit our border in Arizona to observe the problems that exist up front with people crossing over into our country from Mexico unchecked. Kathy was quick to accept the invitation.

My Master and I were playing golf in Arizona for practice and exercise. When he learned that Kathy was coming to the border he asked if he could accompany her on this inspection tour. The Border Patrol people were very gracious and welcomed him wholeheartedly—that meant <u>me</u>, too.

We broke from our golf sessions and scheduled a flight by light airplane from a small airport nearby to a small airport near the border. The flight was to be about and hour and a half in duration.

When we arrived at the charter operation we were met by the pilot who looked like a barnstormer who flew crop-dusters as a side job. He certainly was a crusty old-timer. During his preflight inspection of this little airplane we learned through conversation that he is a long-time charter pilot and flight instructor, having taught many notables as well as others how to fly. It was obvious to me from his thoroughness that he knew what he was doing. He and my Master hit it off quite well.

I was never in a little airplane so once again my learning curve is expanding. When we climbed in my Master sat in the co-pilot's seat on the right side up front and I was tossed along with his hat on the shelf along the seatbacks of the two rear seats. When the pilot opened his side window and shouted "clear" I thought we were about to be hit by something, much like the call of "fore" in the game of golf, called out as a warning to people in the path of a golf ball. I realized as soon as the engine started that the pilot was warning anybody who may be in the proximity of the propeller that he was about to turn it over.

The little puddle jumper managed to get airborne and we were on our way. I could swear I saw the wings flap during take off. En route my Master was allowed to handle the controls in front of him and try his hand at flying the airplane. I knew a new experience was about to develop.

According to the pilot the controls are sensitive and should be handled gently with only enough pressure to guide the airplane in whatever maneuver one wanted it to do. My Master gripped the control column as if it were his driver and we were about to be launched off the tee. Consequently, we were all over the sky. I am glad it is so big and there is plenty of room up here.

We wandered around at various altitudes heading toward our destination. The pilot seemed amused. My Master was having a ball. I was a little seasick, or I guess the term up here is airsick. As we approached the airport the pilot told my Master to release his iron grip on the controls and give him back the airplane so he could land it. The pilot took over, and "greased it on" as they say in aviation lingo.

I hope my Master never decides to someday learn how to fly. A record of that accomplishment put into book form would probably be humorous and worth publishing. As we left our pilot, my Master shook his hand and thanked him for the flying lesson. I thanked him for getting us down in one piece and not bending anything. There is an old saying in aviation that a good landing is any landing that you can walk away from—a great landing is one in which they can use the airplane again. We had a great landing. As we walked away the pilot said to my Master, "If you ever decide to learn how to fly, come see me." My Master said, "Okay." I said, "Forget it."

Kathy met us at this small airport with the Border Patrol who transported us to their headquarters and an orientation session. This reminded me of the military. During the early morning hours there were to be three vehicles departing in a convoy. The first was an observation vehicle which included us. Also in our vehicle were two agents and Kathy's high-ranking lady agent who was in command. The second vehicle contained an apprehension team, and the third a transportation vehicle for anyone apprehended. All vehicles carried night vision binoculars and telescopes and of course all agents are armed.

About two hours before dawn our convoy parked in a small ravine hidden from view but from which a good view of a section of the border could be realized. After about a half an hour through the night vision lenses about a dozen men and women were observed slowly and furtively crossing the border into our country. Once they cleared the border and were well within our country the apprehension team moved in and detained them. The transportation vehicle then went to the scene and we followed.

I could not help but have compassion for these people. Listening to their answers to questions from the border patrol agents upset Kathy. All were penniless and were hoping to find work of any kind. Two of them had been apprehended twice before and sent back to Mexico. Two were extremely dehydrated from lack of water in their long walk to the border on the Mexican side. Still, they persisted hoping to be able to live a decent life in our country. It seems to me that this particular group would make productive citizens here. They merely want a chance to work and exist peacefully. I was saddened by this encounter. So was Kathy and my Master.

Of course a big problem are those who cross our unprotected borders undetected. Many are hardened criminals, drug smugglers and possible terrorists. Kathy fully realizes the gravity of the situation on all counts. There is also a threat to our labor force. The rich are getting richer using the poor and destitute as their springboard and no one holds them accountable. Shame on them.

Kathy feels that no amount of new laws will fix the problem. She considers them only window dressing and will hurt the country in the long run, especially when they probably will never be enforced as in the past. Much clear thinking must go into the solving of this dilemma.

When we left Kathy and my Master thanked the members of the Border Patrol for their courtesy and professionalism. They, too, have a tough mission and yet show a deep concern for those whose lives cross their path. I have come to realize that law enforcement is more than a job—it is more than a profession—it is a way of life. A law enforcement officer can start a shift, and never end it, leaving a grieving family at home. They live with this dreadful reality every day and night. Enough of sad thoughts.

Kathy's lady Border Patrol Commander drove us to a large airport where we boarded a commercial jet home. During the flight I am happy the Captain didn't invite my Master to do some flying. He may be the greatest golfer in the world, but a pilot—maybe I should leave it there.

Kathy is back in Washington now, facing many challenging issues. Her biggest concern is the war and how to end it. Also, there are issues of healthcare, education and Social Security. Veterans hospitals designated to care for our wounded and disabled need a complete makeover. Veterans benefits clearly need to be enhanced with a new commitment to care for veterans' well-being long after their discharge.

Also, the method used to elect the President and Vice-President of the United States had always bothered Kathy. Votes cast by the Electoral College of each state become the decider and not the popular majority vote of those voting. The true voice of the people is not heard. When an election can produce a clear winner by popular vote and this winner becomes the loser by the Electoral College vote there is something inherently wrong. The system was written into law in 1845. It is antiquated. Kathy recognizes that ours is a much different country than it was when our forefathers founded it. This method of voting must be changed for the good of the country. There will come a day when she will do that.

Both Kathy and her senator colleague are on the same page here. Together they are making their legislative mark in Washington, not for personal gain, but for accomplishing meaningful goals. Many legislators from both sides of the aisle are joining in for the good of the country. Decency in politics is catching on and can be contagious. The public is paying attention and loving it.

There are many other issues, the least of which is fiscal responsibility. At the current rate of spending our country will be broke in short order. Clear thinking and not political posturing must go into all of these issues.

With an upcoming presidential election Kathy has been pressured on many sides to declare herself a candidate. Deep thought and many family discussions have taken place.

With her family firmly behind her she decided that when the time came she would make her declaration to run for the Presidency in an unprecedented bipartisan manner. She will announce her Vice-Presidential choice before her party's primary. It will be her wartime senator colleague and friend from the opposition party, if he will accept it.

This will be a true display of bipartisanship. Together they have sponsored many bills which passed muster overwhelmingly. Their record together is impeccable. They have complete trust in one another. Their word is their bond. She will let her party's voters decide in the primary whether or not they want their party and their country to be led in this manner. The nation may have something fresh and new to look forward to. Since she has taken office her efforts have awakened a nation in a political sleepwalk. In the past lobbyists have overrun

Washington. Influence peddling for profit took a hit early on in Kathy's senatorial campaign when she declared all contributions would be turned over to the needy, and they were. With that transparency many lobbyists have gone into other lines of work.

Government is slowly getting back to representing its people fairly. Corporations are losing their grip on legislation. Once again, if I knew how to bet I would bet the farm on her. This may be a true test of this country's willingness to come together in good faith. Most certainly honesty and truthfulness are on her side.

Very soon the news media is destined to go into a feeding frenzy—but what do I know? I'm just a golf ball with powers that amaze even me.

Time will tell.